Molly

A Witch in Time, Saves Nine

by Brian K. Porter
SECOND EDITION

Best wishes to Edward Holmes from Brian Porter. 2/06/05

Published by Barny Books, Hough on the Hill, Grantham, Lincolnshire
Fax: 01400 251737

ISBN Nº: 1 903172 45 4

Produced by TUCANN*design&print*
19 High Street, Heighington, Lincoln LN4 1RG
Tel/Fax: 01522 790009
Email: sales@tucann.co.uk **Website:** www.tucann.co.uk

Molly Perkins lived with her mother and father at 62, Empress Drive. It was an ordinary house in an ordinary row with an ordinary back garden and a front door that opened on to the street. Everything started when her father lost his job. There weren't many orders in the electrical company where he worked and they had to cut down on their staff.

"Last in, first out,", they said and that was Mr Perkins.

"I'm sure something will turn up," Mrs Perkins said.

"I hope you're right dear," Mr Perkins replied. "We've no savings to fall back and it's not easy to get a job at my age," and he dropped his head into his hands in despair.

Mrs Perkins put her arms around his shoulders and gave him a hug. "Come on love," she said, "we've got each other and Molly as well."

"I know. I'll go down town and see if there's any work about when she gets home from school."

That was when the door burst open and Molly rushed in. She always rushed everywhere.

"What's for tea Mum?" She asked throwing her coat and school bag on to the floor . "I'm starving."

She sat down at the table and started to eat before her mother had a chance to say a word.

"It is alright if I go round to Jenny's," she asked between mouthfuls. "She's got a new computer game and I'm longing to have a go on it."

Molly didn't have a computer. Her parents couldn't afford to buy her one but she had lots of friends and they were always ready to share with her. Molly started telling them all that she had done at school that day and there was hardly a chance for her parents to get a word in. Then she pushed the chair back and with, "Won't be long mum," she was out of the door and away.

"That child," tutted Mr Perkins, shaking his head. "Well I'll be off now dear. Perhaps the luck will turn our way one day," and he stepped outside pulling up his collar to protect himself from the rain. He hardly noticed the car draw up and a tall man getting out of it and walking towards him.

"Mr Perkins?" the man asked. "Could I have a word with you?"

"You'd better come back into the house, out of the rain," Mr Perkins said, opening the door and ushering him in.

"I understand Bransons have made you redundant some weeks ago and I know they were sorry to let you go. What are you doing now? Have you found another job?"

"No. I haven't," Mr Perkins said, "I was just off to see if there was anything in town."

"That's why I'm here. I'm friendly with Mr Branson, used to work with him. I need someone and wondered if you would come and work for me," and he explained what he did and what he would want Mr Perkins to do. The only problem was that the job was in Manchester. They would have to move but the firm would pay all their expenses.

"Don't give me an answer straight away. Think about it and let me know."

But Mr and Mrs Perkins did not have to think about it. There had been no other work. By the end of the week, all the arrangements had been made and they were ready to move. Molly hadn't wanted to go. She didn't want to leave her school or her friends and she cried when her parents first told her that they were moving but as she was a sensible girl and she knew how worried and how short of money her parents had been and Jenny said she could come and spend the school holidays with her.

They arrived in Manchester late one evening. It was getting dark. They sat in the van and looked at the house that was to be their new home. The house was big and old and it stood all on its own. There were only four other houses in the street. There had been others but they had been demolished and there were still bricks and steps and pieces of masonry to show where they stood. This road was not like Empress Road with its two rows of terraced houses, neither was this house like the comfortable one they had just left. It looked cold and forbidding with tall windows and tall chimneys. The first thing Molly noticed was the cast iron door knocker in the shape of a lion's head. It seemed to be staring at her and Molly felt a shiver of apprehension run down her spine.

"The first thing I want", said Mrs Perkins in her matter of fact tone, "is a nice cup of tea."

"That's right love. You can't beat a cup of tea. We're going to have fun in this house, you wait and see." Little did he realise at that moment exactly how much fun they would have, especially Molly.

Molly woke up early the next morning but her mother was already up. She could hear her humming as she moved about in her new kitchen. Her father too was pleased with the new house and kept walking round the garden as if he was in a dream but Molly looked out of the window and felt sad. There was a huge expanse of empty land around them where houses had once stood and beyond this space she could see her new school. It looked big and grey and dark, not a bit like the comfortable school she had just lived. How she wished she was back there with all her friends. She didn't want to start there, not one little bit.

"Come on, love," her mother encouraged her, "eat up your breakfast. You'll make lots of new friends. You don't want to be late on your first day do you?"

Oh, but she did. She ate every mouthful as slowly as she could until her mother began to grow impatient.

All the children in the playground seemed to stop what they were doing and turn to stare at Molly and her mother as they made their way across to the school.

"What's your name?" one of them shouted.

"How old are you?" asked another.

"Where are you from?" interrupted a third.

They were surrounded by children and Molly began to feel dizzy.

"O.K., O.K., the show's over. Now scatter," an authoritative voice shouted above theirs and the children spread out, Molly was able to see from where the voice had come. A rather tomboyish figure stood in front of her. "Don't worry about that lot," she said.

"They don't get any excitement in their lives. That's the matter with them. What's your name?"

"Molly."

"Who's class are you in?"

"I don't know yet. We've only just got here."

"Mr Green's office is over there. See you later," and she started walking away.

"I'm Sarah Watts, by the way," she shouted over her shoulder as she disappeared through a doorway.

Molly had to admit that everyone seemed very friendly. She met their secretary and the headmaster and her new teacher introduced her to the children in her class and showed her where she would be sitting. She could hardly believe her luck. Her seat was next to the girl she had met in the playground, Sarah Watts. The two girls became good friends and over the next few weeks Molly learned her way round. There was one thing that worried her and that was a boy called Chunky. His real name was George Hill which nobody, and I mean nobody, would ever dare call him. He was the school bully and everybody was frightened of him. He had been keeping an eye on Molly  from the very first time she had walked through the school gates and he had decided that now was the time to pounce. He stood at the gate, cleaning the dirt from beneath his fingernails with a broken matchstick. He was leaning against the wall and when he saw Molly approaching he stood up in front of her as if to block her pathway.

"Hey little girl, where do you think you're off to."

Molly did not answer him. She moved to the right to pass him. He moved to the right in front of her. She moved to the left. So did he. Molly began to feel frightened. Nothing like this had ever happened to her before.

"Oh my, we are a wriggly little worm, aren't we, a wriggly wiggly worm trying to wiggle off to Mummy," he jeered.

"Leave me alone," Molly stammered.

"Oh listen, it talks, a talking wriggling worm."

He leaned forward so that his face was almost touching hers and she could feel his breath on her cheeks. "No, I won't," he spat at her. "I'm here to make your life hell. That's my mission in life from now on and I'm not going to fail. Do you get me worm?"

"What do you want with me. I've done nothing to you."

"What do you want with me. I've done nothing to you," he taunted her. "What you haven't done, worm, is pay me my protection money, see."

"What do you mean?"

"What I mean is that tomorrow you bring two pounds and give it to me in the playground and that will keep you safe from undesirables and you don't tell no one, see."

He looked round to make sure that nobody was looking and with one swift movement, he punched her in the stomach so hard that Molly doubled up and all the breath was knocked out of her body.

Molly felt sick, sick with the punch to her body and sick with the realisation of what this could mean, a moment she had always dreaded, coming face to face with a bully.

"Come on then," he sneered at her, "where's the money?"

Molly straightened up slowly. Her first instinct was to give him the money. That would make him go away but she knew he would come again. She had to face up to him.

"Get lost," she yelled at him, "and leave me alone.

He was taken aback, but only for a second. He hadn't expected her to retaliate. Nobody answered him back. He reached out and grabbed her collar and slammed her head into the wall as he pushed his face close to hers.

"Think you're tough d'ya," he snarled. "Nobody, I mean nobody argues with Chunky, d'ya hear me, worm?" and there was venom in his voice.

Molly realised she had made a mistake. She should have given in to him.

"Please leave me alone," she pleaded. Chunky was still holding her against the wall. Now he pushed his hand into her pocket.

"Just what I'm looking for," he crowed and letting her go, he delved into the purse. "What a clever worm we have here," he crowed, "two pounds and five for interest. You're better than I thought worm. It's going to be real nice protecting you," and there was something in the way he said that last word that sent a shiver of apprehension down Molly's spine. She put her hand to her face and realised there was blood mixed with the rain and she knew she was hurt. Chunky had emptied the money from the purse and put the coins in his pocket and thrown the purse into the air.

"Please don't take it," Molly pleaded. "that's my dinner money."

"Well you've lost it, haven't you worm. You've lost your dinner money, remember that. There'll be trouble if you say anything different, you'll have to order yourself a coffin." Then he had ambled off whistling with his hands in his pocket.

Molly was shaking. She tried to wipe the blood from her face. Her nose was bleeding and she felt sick. She knew she couldn't go to school in this state so she turned and made for home. Sarah saw her at the end of the road and ran after her.

"Molly," she heard the shock in her voice. "whatever have you done?" Then her voice changed. There was suspicion in her question, "Has someone done this to you because if they have we're going straight up to see Mr Green now."

"No, no," Molly almost pleaded. That would only make things worse. "I fell over."

"What you got hurt like this in a fall?"

"I was running too fast and I tripped and I fell on my nose."

Sarah had her arm round her. She was concerned. She was sure Molly wasn't telling the whole truth. "You will tell me if you're ever in trouble won't you Molly?"

"Of course, I will," Molly answered. "Don't be silly," but she had her fingers crossed tightly so that she could be forgiven for telling a lie.

Sarah walked all the way home with her. Her mother was really concerned when she saw the state her daughter was in. She made her sit down and bathed her face. Molly told her the same story that she had told

Sarah.

"You must be more careful, Molly." She said. The thought that someone could have done this to her never entered her mind. She tucked Molly up in her bed and said that she would phone the school and say that she wasn't going in that day. She asked Molly if she would be alright on her own for an hour because she had to go up to the shops.

"I'll be fine, Mum," she said. "I've just got a bit of a headache."

It was very quiet when her mother had gone. Molly got up and looked out of the window. She could see the school from there and the sight of it brought back all the memories of what had happened to her.

"Why me?" She wailed and threw herself on to her bed and sobbed. Then she lay there full of self pity with her head buried in the pillow.

Tap, tap, tap, Molly heard the noise and sat up wondering what was causing it. There was nothing there but the noise went on, tap ,tap, tap. She thought the sound must be in her head and shook it in an attempt to clear it but the tapping still went on. It was getting on her nerves and she buried her head under the pillow trying to get the noise to go away.

"Hello, are you alright over there? Stop messing around and answer me. I haven't got long you know." The voice was little more than a whisper and it sounded angry.

"Go away," Molly said, still thinking the voices were in her head, "I know you're not really there."

"Oh don't be such a baby. Sit up and listen to me."

"I'm going mad," Molly said aloud. "I know I am."

"No. you're not. It's me. I said I'd be back and here I am. Come and talk to me please but do be quiet."

Molly got up slowly and went and stared at the wall. "What do you want me for?" she asked.

There was no answer.

"This is silly," Molly said. "I'm standing here talking to a wall now. I know I'm going mad."

"Shut up," the voice came again. "I have to keep checking to make sure it's safe to talk."

"What do you mean, safe to talk?" Molly demanded.

"Shhh, keep your voice down," the voice ordered.

"Where are you? Who are you?" Molly demanded.

"My name is Jack," the voice went on with almost a sing song lilt to its words, "and you are Molly."

"Yes," stammered Molly, "but how do you know that. This is weird. I'm sure that George Hill has something to do with this."

"Stop feeling sorry for yourself and listen. Your life is in danger and I need to get out of here to help you and you are the only one who can get me out."

Molly began to feel scared.

"I don't understand. How can I help you?"

"Molly, please listen. Life isn't as bad as you think it is right now but you are in danger and so am I. If you will help me you will put this bully in his place. You can always overcome evil. There's a golden key somewhere in this street. Find it. The sooner you do the bet....," his voice began to trail off.

Molly felt alarmed. "What's happening? What's wrong?"

"Molly, I've got to go. Find...it.......please." His voice faded away.

Molly ran into the bathroom and looked on the other side of the wall but there was no-one there. She ran downstairs and out into the garden. It had stopped raining and it was good to breathe in the fresh air. She needed to put her thoughts in order. This voice had told her that her life was in danger but together they could defeat Chunky Hill, but how. She wished Jenny, her friend in the old school was here with her. She would have understood what was happening. Molly still felt bewildered. How could a wall talk to her. If Jack was real and he could help her, she would have to find this key, the golden key but how did you look for such a small thing in such a long street.

Molly went downstairs and looked out on the road. It had stopped raining and the sun was shining causing the water on the roads to turn into steam so that the cobbled street looked as though it was smoking.

"Where will I find the golden key in this street and what shall I do with it when I find it," she wondered.

Molly went up to her room and looked out of the window. Mrs Towers, their neighbour was standing there and she was looking up at the window. She was looking at her. Molly jumped back. She didn't want to be seen. Mrs Tower's appearance startled her. It seemed that she was being enveloped by the steam that was rising from the road,

It was sweeping and swirling around her until, at times, she was completely hidden but, the thing that shocked Molly most, was her eyes. They were shining like miniature spotlights and they seemed to be piercing the wall, shining straight at her. Then, as Molly peeped from behind the curtains, she picked up two heavy bags and made her way to her house.

Molly shuddered as if she had been hit by a sudden chill. "I've got to stop this," she told herself. "These things can't be happening. Mrs Towers is just a lonely old lady. I must have imagined that her eyes lit up. They couldn't have done that for real. She does give me the creeps though."

Molly wasn't hungry. She pushed the vegetables round the plate when her mother put her tea in front of her. She could only think of everything that had happened to her that day. Her thoughts were miles away when her mother's voice brought her back to reality.

"That's right, dear, isn't it?" Her mother was saying.

"I'm sorry Mum, I didn't catch what you were saying."

"I was telling your Dad about your fall."

"How did you manage that?" Her father asked.

"I was dodging the puddles and I slipped."

"It looks more like you've been hit by a bus than the pavement," her father joked. "Come here and let me give you a big hug."

"Maybe I should tell my Dad everything," Molly thought as she felt herself wrapped in his warm embrace.

"Leave your tea if you don't want it," her mother said. "You took quite a knock."

Molly went up to her room and put the computer game that Jenny had given her on the screen. It was a puzzle and it had taken Molly

14

three weeks to try and solve it but that night everything seemed to go right.

"Yes," Molly shouted out, "yes, I've done it," and there on the screen was a golden key. That was her prize for achieving level two. Molly stared at it hardly believing her eyes. Was this the key that Jack had told her to find? Was this what she wanted to free him from his prison in the wall? She spun round in her swivel chair and stared at the blank wall.

"Jack," she whispered as loudly as she could.

There was no answer.

Molly got up and walked to the wall. "Listen here wall," she said, "I know you can't really talk and that the knock on the head must have made me imagine that you spoke to me this morning. I know you're not for real ," and she stuck her tongue out at the wall. As she turned away, she heard the same loud whispering voice that she had heard that morning.

"Molly, you called. It's me Jack."

Molly spun round and stared at the wall. She couldn't bring herself to speak. She was frozen to the spot with disbelief.

"Who wants me?" The voice continued. "Answer me now." A loud booming noise came from the wall as the tone of the voice changed into a loud roar, "WHO WANTS JACK. TELL ME NOW."

Molly was suddenly frightened. She couldn't answer. She could only think about getting away from that voice and, without another thought in her mind, she turned and raced downstairs.

"Whatever's the matter?" Her mother said, startled by her sudden appearance.

"Didn't you hear all that banging and shouting?" She asked.

"What on earth do you mean, Molly? It's been quiet all evening."

"It hasn't," Molly said. "There's been a voice called Jack shouting at me from the wall. I'm not going to sleep in that room, I'm not."

Mrs Perkins put her arms round her daughter. "You've had a bad dream," she said. "You wait there while I go and see if there's anything there that could have upset you."

She came down after a couple of minutes and said that there was nothing there and she took Molly back upstairs.

"Don't leave me here on my own, please," Molly pleaded. "I'm frightened."

So her mother lay on the bed beside her and the two of them spoke softly until Molly fell asleep. She was woken in the morning by knocking on the front door and someone asking if Molly was going to school. "It's Sarah," Molly called downstairs. "Can she come up, Mum?"

Sarah was shocked to see Molly's face.

"Do I look that bad?" Molly asked.

"No, well yes you do. Are you sure you just fell over?" Before Molly could answer, Sarah started to tell her a secret.

"I've got a better secret than that," Molly told her and told her about Jack and the talking wall and the search for the golden key.

"That's exciting," Sarah said. "We've got to find it."

"Aren't you frightened?" Molly asked.

"Course I'm not. We must find the key. It'll be in the street somewhere but this is a funny street."

"What do you mean," Molly asked her, "a funny street?"

"Well it is a funny street. There's always people moving in here, then, well they just disappear. I better go to school now, but I'll come and see you tonight. Ask your Mum if I can stay."

The day dragged for Molly. In the afternoon she went and watched from her bedroom window until she saw Sarah making her way through the allotments. Her mother had phoned Sarah's to ask if she could stay the night. It seemed the evening would never come but there was Sarah, at last, and she was carrying a bag that looked really heavy as if she had packed enough for one month rather than a night. Molly ran downstairs and opened the door for her.

"Hi," Sarah said, " I think I've got everything I'll need. Now where's the key?"

"Sh," Molly hushed. "Mum'll hear."

They made their way upstairs and settled on the rug on the bedroom floor.

"I hope Jack'll speak tonight," Sarah said. "I want to hear his voice. Now tell me again everything that happened. You say this Mrs Towers is a bit suspicious. I reckon we must go and search her house."

"We can't do that," Molly said. "We don't want to get into trouble but there is something odd about her. She's weird."

"Then we'll start with her," Sarah said in a matter of fact way. "We'll put her under surveillance. You know like the police do in films. We watch her house to see who goes in and out."

They must have stood for the best part of an hour standing at the window, staring at Mrs Tower's house and they didn't see anyone go in or out.

"This surveillance is getting boring. Let's go and do something else."

"Wait a minute," Sarah replied. "Someone's coming along the road now."

"That is Mrs Towers. It looks as though she's been shopping. She does seem to do a lot of shopping."

"Let's go and help her," and Sarah jumped down the stairs with Molly close behind her.

"Can we carry your bags for you, Mrs Towers, " she offered, when they reached her.

Mrs Towers seemed a bit startled. "I suppose so," she said and the girls picked up a bag each and walked beside her to her house.

"You better come in," the old lady said as she fumbled with her key. Then, as she opened the door, she asked Molly if she could put the shopping in her kitchen for her. Both girls made for the kitchen door but Mrs Towers called out, "not you dear, just Molly."

The girls looked at each other and Sarah went back into the room. Molly followed her when she had left the shopping on the kitchen table. Mrs Towers was standing in the middle of the room and there was a strange look on her face. "You've seen something, haven't you, in that house. I knew he'd come back one day. I knew it," and she burst into tears. "Make me a cup of tea, dear, will you and I'll tell you all about it."

"This used to be a good street," Mrs Towers started when Molly had handed her a cup of tea. Children used to play along the pavements, laughing and calling out. It's all gone now. It's those memories that hurt. I'm what you call white you know," she added in a whisper. "A white witch. Don't be alarmed dear. There are the good witches and the bad ones. Keep away from the bad ones. You'll know which they are."

She went on talking in this way for an hour or more while the cup of tea on the table grew cold. She kept talking about the happy days when the children played in the street and about her own son who played with them. Then one day he had gone to play with his friend Peter who lived in the house where Molly lived now and he had never come out.

"There's evil in that house," she said. "Evil I'm telling you, evil." She stopped talking and stared straight ahead.

The two girls sat staring at her. They were fascinated and frightened.

"Did you know anyone called Jack, Mrs Towers?" Molly asked.

"Jack, he's my son. Have you seen him? Have you spoken to him? Look, there's a photo of him on the mantelpiece," and she stood up and reached a framed photo from the shelf and showed it to the girls. "I don't have the powers that I used to have. I can't help you. Be careful. What did my Jack say to you?"

"He said something about finding a golden key."

"And was there another voice? Did anyone else speak?"

"There was another voice but I couldn't understand it. It was deep and it, it was frightening. I didn't like it."

"It's him. He's back," Mrs Towers was almost shouting. "It's starting all over again." Then, lowering her voice, she went on, "You can't go back there. It's too dangerous for you. He searches for young souls to feed on. When he has found them, he becomes stronger than ever."

The old lady's eyes were wide open and she was staring at a spot on the wall in front of her. She seemed to have forgotten that the two girls were there.

"The golden key, Mrs Towers," Molly almost shouted at her. "Do you know where we can find the golden key?"

Mrs Towers blinked and seemed to come back to life again.

"I do have a little power left, she said, "but it gets weaker every time I use it, but we'll see," and she went across to the corner cupboard and took out a big, heavy box from which she lifted a large crystal ball. She placed it carefully in the middle of the table. She sat down on a chair beside the table and concentrated on the ball and slowly her eyes closed and, as they closed, the crystal ball seemed to come to life. It shone with an increasing brilliance that made the rest of the room seem dull and lifeless until a smaller, purple ball seemed to develop in the centre of the ball and it moved round the globe as if trying to escape. Then it was circling above their heads, hovering, turning, twisting. Then it moved towards the door and the door opened to let it through but the purple ball twisted and danced and bobbed in the doorway before moving on.

"Come on," said Molly, "it's telling us to follow."

The ball of light was moving quickly now and the girls had to run after it as it went towards the old stone wall at the end of the street and then it simply disappeared into the stone. And where it had entered the wall. The stones seemed to move and one of them fell to the ground and in the cavity that was left was a small packet, tied with string.

Molly bent and picked it up. "Open it, Molly," Sarah urged her

but Molly didn't have to unwrap it. The paper was so old that it crumbled in her hands and there was a key, a golden key.

"It's the key. It's the key," Molly said excitedly. "Come on, let's go and tell Mrs Towers."

But when they reached the room where they had left her, there was no sign of the old lady. She had disappeared into thin air and the crystal ball had exploded into a thousand pieces that littered the ground and seemed to be moving. The light reflecting on the broken pieces seemed to stir and jostle the shards until the furniture in the room seemed to be shaking too and the walls and the ground and the children themselves felt unsteady.

"Quick," said Sarah, "we must get out of here."

As they ran out of the front door, the whole house started to shake and then, with what seemed like a huge sigh, the building collapsed, crashing in clouds of dust. The girls stared at it in disbelief. Then, as the dust settled, they saw this object on top of the rubble.

"It's Mrs Tower's shopping bag," Molly said, "the one I put on the kitchen table. Look, there's some writing on it. Can you see what it says. Can you read it?"

"I'm trying to but it's not very clear, - SOLVE THE PUZZLE ON THE KEY. THEN AND ONLY THEN CAN YOU SET MY SON FREE.. What does it say on the key?"

"I can't make it out. It's all jumbled up," Molly said.

"Let me look," Sarah said, pushing Molly out of the way but she couldn't make head or tail of it either.

Then they were disturbed by a siren and a police car followed by a fire engine. An ambulance roared up and a crowd of people seemed to appear from nowhere to watch the rescuers sift through the rubble. It began to get dark and they brought up lamps so they could see where they were digging. Mrs Perkins came out to fetch the girls in. It was time for them to get ready for bed.

"Do you think our house is safe?" Molly whispered to Sarah.

"Course it is," Sarah said. "Your mother's not a witch is she."

That made Molly laugh to think of her mother flying round on a broomstick.

It was after Mrs Perkins had been up to settle them down for the night that the two girls began to discuss the day's events and try and sort out the peculiar code on the golden key.

It read, - EM ROF ROOD A EKAM UOY DNAMED I 2 YE KEHT FOR E DLO HEHT MA I 1.

"It's got to mean something, but what?" Molly said with a sigh.

"Why don't you let your computer work it out." Sarah suggested.

"Brilliant," Molly said. "Why didn't I think of that?" She tapped the letters into the computer and waited.

The computer worked away but it didn't seem to be coming up with anything useful.

"Let me have a look," Sarah said and she slid onto Molly's swivel chair. "It's here Molly. You need a mirror, see. Everything is written back to front. It comes out alright if you look in the mirror."

"Why didn't I think of that. Move over Sarah, we can both sit on the chair. I can see now. Hang on while I write it down on the pad."

It came out 2 I DEMAND YOU MAKE A DOOR FOR ME.

1 I AM THEH OLD E ROF THEKEY

"I can understand the first line but...."

"Here, let me look," said Sarah. "It's easy. You just have to move the letters round a bit. I am the holder of the key. It's as clear as a pikestaff."

"What do we do now?"

"See if you can call Jack up."

So Molly stood in the centre of the room with the key held tightly in her hand and repeated the words that were written on it.

It didn't work. The girls stood still for five minutes without moving or talking but nothing happened..

"I know what the problem is," Molly said suddenly. "We're saying it backwards. We should say number one first then number two. Let's try that."

So they repeated the words but this time Molly chanted the statements in that order and, as she finished speaking, there was a whoosh and a door appeared in the wall at the exact spot from which she had heard Jack's voice. It gave Molly such a shock that she dropped the key and, straight away, the door disappeared.

"Did you see that Sarah?"

"You're not kidding." Sarah stood there with her mouth open in astonishment, staring at the spot where the door had appeared and, just as quickly, disappeared." I reckon that whoever is holding the key can make the door appear," she said.

The two of them stood there staring at the blank wall. Should they aim the key in that direction again or should they wait for Jack to give them a signal.

Mrs Perkins settled the matter. She was getting cross with the two girls. It was time they were asleep. She didn't know what they were getting up to but, whatever it was, it was time it was finished and they both settled down. As soon as she had gone downstairs again and they couldn't hear her moving about the two girls sat up.

"What shall we do now?" Molly whispered. She didn't want her mother to hear them. "Shall we wait for Jack?"

"We could bring the door up again and go through it to see where it goes," Sarah suggested.

"Are you crazy? There could be all kinds of dreadful things on the other side but," and Molly paused to think, "it is tempting."

But it was then that something very strange happened. Mrs Perkins had turned out the light when she'd left the room, Now Molly said that she was going to turn the light on and as soon as the words left her mouth, the light came on, - on its own.

"It's the key," Molly said. "It understands what I say. I was holding it when I said I was going to turn the light on and it did it for me."

"Can I have a go?" Sarah asked and, reaching out, she took the key from her friend. Molly could hear her under the bedclothes giving the key orders but nothing seemed to happen.

"It's not happening for me," she said, sounding disappointed.

Magic things will only work for the first mortal that touches them and that, of course, had been Molly but Sarah didn't realise that and she tried all sorts of words to get it to work for her.

"I'll try it again, in my left hand this time. She told the key to turn out the light and immediately it went out."

"There you are," Sarah said. "It's you it wants but I shouldn't care. We're in this together. It doesn't matter if you give the orders."

The other thing that neither of the girls realised was that the more the mortal held the magic possession such as the key, so more of its power was transferred to the mortal. But there is one other thing they didn't know and that was that the power they had must only ever be used for good and to fight off evil. Molly didn't realize this but she did feel herself growing more and more confident.

"I think we'll wait until tomorrow night if Jack doesn't turn up," Molly said.

"That's fine," Sarah said. "That'll give us time to sort things out and decide what we want to take with us. We don't know what we'll find on the other side of the door."

"Molly, hello."

Something was happening. Molly felt a warm tingling sensation making her feel pleasant and warm. It was as if her whole body was giggling.

"Hey, Molly, what's happening to you?" Sarah asked. "You look different. All the bruises on your face have gone."

"I know. Isn't it great. I feel fantastic," and she started to laugh.

Sarah tried to make her stop. "You'll have your mother up here again if you're not quiet," she said.

"D'you know Sarah. I'm going back to school tomorrow," Molly said between her giggles. "I've some unfinished business to deal with."

"What sort of business?" Sarah asked suspiciously.

"You'll see," and she tapped the key on her other hand. "You'll see."

Mrs Perkins was up bright and early the next day but so were Sarah and Molly. They were downstairs, ready for school while Mr Perkins was still eating his breakfast. Mrs Perkins generally had a snooze in a chair after her husband had left for work and before she called Molly down for breakfast, but not that day. She couldn't believe the difference in her daughter.

"It's this new friend of hers," she thought, "I knew she would be good for her."

The girls left for school before eight o'clock. The workmen were already clearing the rubble from the demolished house. The noise of the digger and the workmen calling out and whistling made Molly think of Mrs Towers and the message they had found on the shopping bag. Then she thought of Jack and wondered what he would be like.

Sarah told Molly to wait outside the paper shop while she ran home and saw her Mum to ask her if it was alright to stay at Molly's for another night. "I'll catch you up," she said.

Molly carried on walking. "If that big bully shows his face today, he'd better watch out because I'm ready for him," Molly said to herself. She turned the corner to the paper shop and looked carefully up and down. There was no sign of Chunky but, as she reached the newsagents, she saw him coming up the road. Their eyes met and she saw that stupid grin spread across his face as he started to walk towards her and she knew he meant business. She quickly felt into her bag and fumbled for the key, but she couldn't find it. Then it was too late. He had reached her and stood so close to her that she couldn't get away from him and his breath blew into her face. He grabbed Molly by her chin and pressed his finger and thumb into her jaw forcing her head back and making her feel sick. The pain was excruciating. He pushed her head further back and her legs buckled.

"What are you doing this for. You're hurting."

"Shut up worm," he said. "You didn't make it before so you owe me double today."

"I haven't any money. You took it all."

"Shut up, worm. I'll tell you when you can speak."

Then Sarah appeared round the corner and she shouted at Chunky telling him to let Molly alone. He gave her a punch on the side of her face. "See you later," he said, "don't think I've finished with you," and he am-

bled off down the road.

"So that was how you fell over," Sarah said. "You could have told me the truth. He's evil, he is, a real bully. You want to keep away from him."

"Don't tell Mum will you Sarah. Promise."

"Course I won't. We'll deal with him ourselves."

Molly was still looking in her bag. "I can't find the key," she said. "I'm sure I put it in my bag."

"You didn't. You put it mine by mistake. Here, put it round your neck on a chain or something then you'll know where it is. Did that bully get any money off you, by the way."

"I didn't have any to give him. He took all I had the other day."

"You should have told your Mum you know. He needs stopping that boy does. He's sick, he is. Still we'll sort him out," and the two of them went into school laughing and discussing what they could do to Chunky Hill.

Home time couldn't come soon enough. The two girls kept wondering if they would get in touch with Jack that evening. As they walked out of the school gates, Molly caught sight of Chunky. He looked as though he was waiting for her or perhaps he was searching out some other victim. Molly looked straight at him. She held on to Sarah's arm for comfort and, with her free hand she delved into her bag for the key. As she looked at him, letters began to appear on his face, letters that had been tattooed there and would never fully disappear. "I love Molly Perkins," they read.

Chunky began to feel uncomfortable. He couldn't see the words on his face and he wondered why everyone was looking at him. "What are you all looking at," he shouted, "sod off," and he pushed through the crowd of children coming out of the gates and ran off.

"Just wait until he sees what's written on his face," Molly laughed.

"And guess what he'll be like when he tries and wash it off." Sarah added.

Chatting and laughing the two girls made their way home. After tea, they hurried upstairs and settled in Molly's room. They sat on the floor, patiently waiting for Jack to appear or, at least, say something to let them know he was there.

"Do you think he will come?" Sarah asked.

"I don't know," Molly said and she walked across to the wall. She put her face very close to it and whispered, "Come on Jack. Where are you? We're waiting for you. Give us a sign."

Nothing happened. There wasn't a sound except for the clock loudly ticking the seconds and minutes away. Molly went across and stood at the window looking out. There was nothing there, nothing moved except for dead leaves that were being tossed by the wind.

There were three street lights that cast shadows across the road. One of them was right outside the spot where Mrs Tower's house had been but now it was just a bare patch of ground, indistinguishable from the rest of the flattened street. It was impossible to believe that only the day before, a house had stood on that very spot.

"It must have been a real nice street at one time," Molly said. "I wonder if Mrs Towers had lived here all her life. How old would you say she was?"

"Very, I think," Sarah said. "She had a lot of wrinkles. Look Molly, I think you'll have to bring that door up again and we'll have to go and look for Jack."

The two girls sat on the bed and looked into the bags and the things they had packed into them ready for this journey into the unknown. Molly had picked up a torch and was holding it when Sarah noticed it was flashing on and off like a car's indicator.

"You'll flatten the battery if you let it flash like that," Sarah told her.

"But I haven't touched it," Molly said. "I'm only holding it."

The two girls looked at each other. Something strange was happening. Perhaps Jack was there after all.

"I wasn't holding the key," Molly said.

"But you've got it on the chain round your neck and that's the same thing," Sarah answered.

It was the first thing the girls had done when they got home and that was to look through her mother's old jewellery box for a piece of chain and they had found a silver length that was just the right size. They had slipped the key on to it and fastened the chain round Molly's neck. She wouldn't lose the key again.

"Go on, Molly, try something else," Sarah urged her.

"I'm going to open the door."

"Which door?" Sarah asked.

"The bedroom door of course," and she just looked in its direction. A twitch of her nose and the door knob began to turn slowly then, without warning, - Wham - the door flew open.

"It's scary," Sarah began. Then she looked at Molly's eyes. They were bright and shining and piercing.

"Your eyes," she said, "they're like Mrs Towers were. Molly, you're becoming a witch."

Molly looked at herself in the mirror. "I'm scared Sarah," she said. "This is really freaky."

"Don't be," Sarah said. "Think of all the things you can do. You could fly or turn things into stone. We can have some good fun at school. Just think of it. Ooh, my friend, a witch."

It was nine o'clock. Mrs Perkins had been up and settled the girls down for the night. "Now not too much talking," she said as she went out.

"I don't reckon he's coming now," Sarah said.

"Well this is it," Molly said. "We'll have to go and look for him," and she stood facing the wall with the key in her hand.

"I am the holder of the key,
I demand you make a door for me," she began.

Whoosh. There it stood right before their eyes, a solid wooden door with two bright brass hinges fastened to the wall. Half way down was a brass lock waiting for the key to be inserted and turned. Molly's hand trembled as she lined up the key and slowly eased it into the keyhole. Sarah was close behind her. As she turned the key, a large brass door knob appeared. Sarah tried to pull it but the door didn't budge.

"You'll have to help me, Molly. It's really heavy."

The two girls took hold of it and pulled with all their might. There was a long, drawn out creaking and slowly the door began to open.

Then the girls felt themselves falling through the doorway and then it slammed shut on them and disappeared. They sat up and looked around them,

"This is freaky. We're back in your bedroom. Everything's exactly the same. Look there's your shoes and your school bag just where you left it."

"Yes and there's your book and biro," Molly said as she got to her feet. What

the girls had not realised was that this room was an exact copy of Molly's own bedroom, right down to the smallest detail.

Molly went across to the window to look out on to the street. There were rows and rows of trees like a coloured rain forest. "Come and look at this," she called out to Sarah.

Her friend stood beside her at the window. "Where have they all come from? What has happened to the street? I don't like this Molly. Let's get back through the door. Get that key working." Sarah was beginning to panic.

Molly pulled the key out and repeated the chant. Nothing happened. She tried it several times but the door failed to appear and the girls stood staring at the blank wall. Sarah started to bang on the wall in frustration, hitting it with both her fists. She turned and looked at Molly. Her friend's eyes were glowing again.

"Aren't you scared too?"

"I was, but I'm not now. I've got this warm feeling coming over me again," and she began to giggle. "Look behind you now."

Sarah turned to look at the wall that she had been banging and there, written up in golden letters was the verse,

FIND YOUR WAY ABOUT
TO FIND THE SNEOTS TO LET YOU OUT.

FIND YOUR WAY ABOUT
TO FIND THE SNEOTS TO LET YOU OUT

"Whatever is a sneot?" Sarah asked, "It sounds like someone with a cold. I don't think we'll ever get out of here. We're done for."

"We'd better do as the clue says. Come on Sarah, we'll be alright," Molly comforted her. "Now where's that writing pad?" She said as she made her way across to the dressing table. If this table is an exact copy of mine, it should be in the second drawer down. Here it is."

Sarah gave her a half chewed pencil and Molly wrote the message down but she was only just in time because the letters had been fading and, as she wrote the last letter, they completely disappeared.

"See what you can make of that," she said handing the pad to Sarah. "You're the puzzle wizard."

Sarah studied the paper, turning it upside down and sideways on. "This doesn't make much sense," she said, " steons, stonse, I've got it, it's stones of course."

"Good, " Molly said. "Tear that page out and give it to me."

She took the torn page and put it her back pocket. As she did so, the bedroom door flew open with a loud whoosh. It startled the two girls. It was so unexpected. Molly felt the presence of someone in the room with them. There was someone standing behind them and the presence made her feel frightened. Slowly, she turned round and found herself facing the figure of a young boy, a boy about their own size and age. She had seen this boy before, in the photo that Mrs Towers

had shown them. She gripped Sarah's arm tightly.

"You're Jack aren't you?" she asked.

His eyes lit up. "No...no...time to.... explain. Follow me. Come....quickly. Come on now before it is too late." He was pointing towards the door and he was panting.

The two girls reacted immediately and found themselves running down a long passage behind him, lined with old fashioned torches at regular intervals that cast moving waves of light and shadows against the roughly cut stone. They seemed to be hurrying through a labyrinth with the tunnel turning first one way, then the other. Then they turned left and found themselves facing a heavy wooden door. The boy

29

pushed it open revealing a flight of stone steps.

"Hurry up, down the stairs," he said. "Quickly before we are spotted."

"Spotted by who," Sarah gasped as they struggled to keep up with the boy.

"No... time... to ... explain," he said breathlessly.

Molly looked at Sarah. She was flushed and panting. "Are you alright?" She asked.

"I'm shattered," she said, "and this bag seems to be getting heavier."

"How much further?" Molly said to the boy.

"Keep up with me," the boy repeated, "keep up with me until it's safe."

They seemed to be descending the stairs for ages but it gave Molly time to think and grow doubtful. Was this boy really Jack? Where were they being taken? What was going to happen to them? She reached out and pinched Sarah.

"What did you do that for?" Her friend demanded indignantly.

"Sarah, get ready to run back up the stairs. I've got this feeling, a strange feeling that something is going to happen."

"Molly! Stop it will ya, your frightening me."

At that moment the boy stopped. It was almost as if he was reacting to Molly's thoughts. The two girls came to a halt behind him. The boy was changing. He was undergoing a transformation. His whole body was shaking. His head doubled in size, steadily growing larger until his jaw split in two. His body was changing as well, swelling and growing into the shape of a spear and at the same time his clothes tore away and hair began to grow in their place, long black hairs making him look more like and insect than a boy. Molly was crawling back up the stairs scrambling to get away from this creature trying to pull Sarah with her but Sarah was transfixed with the scene unfolding before her and she broke away, screaming in such panic that the sound echoed and re-echoed along the tunnel.

The boy's transformation was now complete. He had changed into a huge, black, hairy spider. His jaws started snapping and with his long hairy legs, he started to mount the steps behind the girls. Its eyes glowed red in the gloomy light of the tunnel and his head swung from side to side in a menacing way. Then, without warning, it began to scurry up the stairs after them, coming faster and faster. For

tunately the two of them had had a good start and they had nearly reached the top step with this menacing creature advancing on them all the time, when the door at the top swung to with a slam. Sarah rushed at it and tried to push it open but it didn't budge. "Molly," she called out with panic in her voice. "The door won't open. It's jammed."

The dreadful spider was almost upon them and Sarah was kicking at the door in an attempt to open it.

"Don't worry," Molly said in a calm voice. "We will make our own. Stand to one side." Her hands fumbled as she felt for the key. Out of the side of her eyes, she could see that the giant spider was almost upon them and she struggled to hold the key. Then, just in time, the door swung open and there was a silhouette of a figure standing on the other side. "Come with me," it said and, without pausing to think, the two girls rushed through the door towards him. And, at that moment Sarah felt something catching hold of her, she felt the thing that had touched her sliding down her back and she knew the spider had reached them. She screamed and stumbled over the threshold and as they went into the passage on the other side, the door swung silently to behind them and Sarah's scream was taken up by a scream on the other side of the door and they saw with a shock that the door had trapped two of the giant spider's feet, cutting them so that the blood spread across the ground.

"Phew," went Sarah and sank on to the ground, "that was something else.."

"You're Molly aren't you?" The silhouette said.

"Who wants to know?" Molly asked cautiously.

"It's me Jack."

"I thought that, that thing was Jack."

"I really am Jack, honestly."

Molly stood looking at him suspiciously. He certainly looked like the photo that Mrs Towers had showed them but so had that other boy and look what had nearly happened last time. "If you really are Jack, who was that thing behind there?" she asked.

"That was one of Peter's little creations," Jack told her.

"Little? Little? If that was little I wouldn't want to be around for his biggest. This is my friend, Sarah by the way."

"Pleased to meet you Sarah," Jack said politely. "We mustn't stand around here talking. We must find a safe place, come on. I'll explain later. Keep your voices down. Sound travels quickly underground."

"He's a bossy git," Sarah whispered to Molly as they followed Jack back along the tunnel. They ran along a series of tunnels one leading out from another and up and down countless steps until they finally stopped. All three of them were panting with the exertion

"Jack," Molly said, "you have some explaining to do. What is this place? Where are we?"

"I reckon we're somewhere under the old street."

"Then why can't we dig our way out." Interrupted Sarah.

"I wish we could but it's not as easy as that. You see the whole area down here is like protected by a wall, an invisible wall. You can't see it but it's there just the same. Nothing can penetrate it. The only way out is by the way you came in. I've been running round these tunnels for years trying to get back to the real world."

"How old is he then Moll?" Sarah whispered but Jack heard her.

"Look at your watches and tell me what the exact time is," he said.

Sarah looked at her watch, tapped it and looked at it again. It had stopped at the second the two of them had walked through the door from Molly's bedroom. "I must have knocked it on the way in," she said. "It's stopped."

"I must have knocked mine at the same time then," said Molly showing Sarah her watch. It looks as though we've been down here for no time at all but we've been here for ages."

"There's no such thing as time down here. Everything has been created by that evil Peter and the key," Jack told them.

"But we saw trees out of the bedroom window," Molly said.

"You probably did. Anything is possible in that room but believe me, down here, you are trapped in time." He sat down and put his head in his hands. "I don't know how long I've been down here but it seems for ever. I bet my parents are both dead by now."

Molly put her arm round Jack's shoulders to comfort him "Is your surname Towers?" she asked.

"How did you know that?" The boy asked.

"We spoke to your Mum before we came through the door."

"She's still alive, I might be able to see her again."

"Not exactly Jack, you see she helped us find the key and then, well then she disappeared."

"Well she could still be alive, disappearing isn't the same as being dead," and he grinned at them both.

"Come to that," Molly said, "how did you know my name?"

"I told you, sound travels fast down here."

"Well why did you say my life was in danger. What did you mean?"

"He wasn't wrong there, Molly," Sarah said, "look what nearly happened to us."

"It's a long story," Jack said. "You were and you still are in danger, grave danger. You have the key, haven't you?"

"Yes but...."

"He knows, Molly. Peter knew as soon as you came through the door, when the bedroom changed its contents. It all started a long time ago," and he told them how Peter had once lived in the house where Molly lived now. One day he had shown Jack the golden key with strange letters on it and, when he had it in his hand, he could do magic and he created horrible things. Then he had found out what the words said and he had made the door appear on the wall in the same way that Molly had done and the two boys had gone through it. But Peter had been in such a hurry that he had left the key in the lock and the door had slammed to behind them. They had found themselves in a room that was exactly the same as the one they had just left even down to the bag of marbles on the dressing table. In all the time that they had been there, nobody had ever been to the other side of the wall. Peter had gone crazy and used his evil powers to make the tunnels and dreadful monsters that prowled in them and Jack had spent all these years hiding in them.

"I don't know who took the key and hid it but it was obviously someone who didn't want to let it get into the wrong hands. If only I had listened to my father, I would never have found myself in this fix. He warned me about Peter and told me not to go into his house but I didn't listen to him."

At that moment there was a loud bang like an explosion. The three children jumped up. "Come on," said Jack, "we've got to get away from here. He knows about the key and he'll do anything to get it."

Jack led them through another door and along yet another corridor. They seemed to be going further and further into the labyrinth. Sarah was surprised to see so many flaming torches and realised that it must be magic at work to make them shine so brightly.

Sarah was beginning to limp. She wished she had been wearing her trainers and not these new shoes. They were rubbing a sore spot on her heel. She was finding it difficult to keep up with the others and lent on the wall to reach down and try to make her shoe more comfortable. She was standing beneath one of these torches and, as she put her hand out to steady herself, she felt something touch it. She glanced up and froze with horror. There was a snake, smooth and shining, disappearing into the burning torch like a long tongue. As she looked, it turned and a single eye stared straight back at her.

"Come on Sarah, get a move on. There's no time to be hang around," Molly shouted back at her and, at the same time, the snake hissed at her, "Go on, we're waiting for you." Sarah was startled.

She hurried to catch up with them, looking at every torch she passed, wondering if each one hid a snake like the one she had seen.

"Quick, through here," Jack whispered. They turned down another corridor and came to another door which Jack pushed open and they were back in a bedroom.

"How have we got back to the bedroom," Molly asked sounding bemused, "we must have gone round in circles."

"Molly, it's not the same bedroom, believe me. It may look the same but it isn't the same room," Jack insisted. "There are a lot of these rooms and they all look the same, it's a kind of joke that Peter plays. He's making them all the time."

"Well what do we do now?"

Jack pointed at the bed and they sat on the edge of it while he told them how he had managed to stay alive all these years. Because the bedrooms had been the same, they had provided good hiding places.

Then Sarah pointed at the writing pad in the middle of the bed. "Look, Molly, it's just where you threw it. D'you remember?"

"Let me look at it," Molly said. "That proves it. This must be the same room. Where's the page I tore out of it?" and she looked straight at Jack.

He stood up and started to pace the room. Then he turned and faced the girls. "Listen carefully, he said. "Things in this place like the sky outside the window. One minute it's sunny and the next, you hear thunder. If you move anything about in one of these bedrooms, then exactly the same thing happens in the others. Now if you take something from an object, that part of it stays in the room, but it will stay complete in the other rooms."

"So all we need to do is to find the bedroom with a piece torn out of the writing pad," said Sarah.

"That's right, but in the meantime, we have to stay in front of Jack until we do find the right room and that might take ages and ages."

"I wonder if the words I wrote down will help," Molly said and she reached into her pocket and took out the torn piece of paper. "It's blank," she exclaimed. "The words have disappeared. Well that was a waste of time. I definitely wrote them down didn't I Sarah?"

"It doesn't surprise me," Jack said. "Nothing surprises me down here. There's one thing that's good about it and that is you wrote it down. Can you remember what was written on the paper?

Molly closed her eyes and thought, then she repeated the rhyme.
FIND YOUR WAY ABOUT
TO FIND THE STONES TO LET YOU OUT.

"Well, there are plenty of stones down here," Jack said. "How many do we need?" but none of them knew the answer to that.

Suddenly Molly felt uneasy. She felt another presence and it was very close.

"Quiet ," she said and they sensed the urgency in her voice and stood perfectly still. They all heard them, footsteps and they were getting closer. They were coming towards them.

"It's him. It's evil Peter," said Jack. There was fear in his voice.

"Molly, do something," Sarah yelled, "You're supposed to be the witch."

"No, give me a hand with the wardrobe. Hurry, there's no time to waste," Jack said.

But Molly stood staring at the door. Sarah knew that she was going to do something when she saw her eyes start to glow. The door slammed shut with a bang that reverberated round the room. Bolts appeared all down one side. "Clack, clack, clack," they sounded as they slid across one after the other, holding the door fast. Molly spun round and pointed towards the wardrobe and, as she pointed, it slid silently to one side revealing a hole, big enough for them to clamber through one after the other.

Sarah went through first and, as she disappeared, something started banging on the locked door, banging so violently that the whole room seemed to shake.

"I know you're in there and I know you've got my key. It's mine and I must have it. I'm going to rip your hearts out and feed them to my pets."

"Quick, Molly, get through," Jack pointed at the hole and she quickly followed her friend. Jack went to follow her and it was at that instant that the door finally gave way and she could hear the roar as the pursuer made for him. Jack was half in and half out of the hole. Molly seized hold of his arms and pulled frantically, trying to pull him through. Evil Peter roared with anger. He reached out his arms. Balls of fire blasted from his claw like fingers as he made for the hole. Molly retaliated by throwing stones through the hole towards him. Somehow Jack managed to scrabble through the last inches and join the girls but they knew that evil Peter was not far behind them.

"Pinch me and tell me I'm dreaming and that this isn't really happening," Sarah said.

"Keep moving," Jack shouted at her. "Keep your energy for your legs."

"But Molly had turned and was staring at the hole. Her eyes were glowing brightly and, as she stared, the stones that were scattered on the ground collected together and filled the hole. Molly carried on staring at them, her eyes seeming to bore into them. They fused together and set hard like concrete.

"That'll hold him for a while," Molly said, "now let's get the hell out of here."

They ran. They dodged the holes that peppered the ground and scrambled over shallow walls that stood in their way. Then a chill entered Molly's body again and she sensed the presence of the evil one once more. And the feeling grew stronger. She knew that Peter was gaining on them. She turned and faced the way they had come. What would his evil mind think of doing now, she wondered.

"Molly, what are you stopping for?" Sarah shouted. She and Jack were some way in front of her and they were leaning on the wall trying to regain their breath.

"It's O.K." She called out to them. "I know what's coming."

"But there's nobody there."

Then they saw the figure caught at the far end of the tunnel, a figure that was old and twisted, his eyes sunk deep into his skull. Long fanged teeth hung down from his upper jaw.

It was him. It was Peter, the evil one. For the first time, Molly stood face to face with him.

Sarah screamed and hid her face in Jack's chest. Molly focused her eyes on this evil thing, eyes that pierced the air like laser beams. The apparition kept his distance but not his temper. He ranted and raged, snarled and chanted at Molly.

"Come on then," said Molly with scorn in her voice. "I've had enough of you. Bullies like you need to be taught a lesson. The time has come to stand and fight back."

Molly stared at the roof and the rocks began to fall, slowly at first, then they were tumbling down at such a speed that they overtook the threatening, evil creature. The dust billowed towards them in a dense cloud, spreading like a thick fog. Then, suddenly everything stopped, the noise, the movement of falling rocks, the dust. It was as if someone had flicked a switch and the world had stopped. They stood in a vacuum.

Sarah was the first to speak. "That was close, Molly. You certainly showed him who was boss,"

The three of them stood there as if collecting their thoughts and it was then that something rolled out from the rubble, something that shone and sparkled. Molly bent down and picked it up carefully. She had never seen anything like it before. Then she saw that the letter B had been engraved on it. She gently rubbed the stone with the sleeve of her sweat shirt. "I wonder what B stands for," she said. Then, turning it over, it said, "Find another eight just like me."

"It's one of the clues," Sarah said. "We must find another eight crystals, - nine crystals, nine letters. We're looking for a nine letter word. Now that evil Peter is dead, we can concentrate on finding the words."

"We can't be sure that he's dead," Jack said. "We don't know that he is for sure."

"No normal person could have survived that rockfall." Sarah stated.

"Well he isn't is he? He isn't normal."

Molly placed the crystal carefully in her bag and the three of them carried on along the tunnel until they found themselves facing an old, rusty, cast iron gate. It spanned the whole width of the tunnel. On the other side of the gate was another tunnel which ran horizontally to the one they were in.

"Do we go left or do we go right?" Molly asked.

Jack shrugged. He had never been along here before so it didn't matter which way they went. He started to push the gate but it was so old and the rust was so solid that it could have been welded together. Molly pushed her head through the rails of the gate to see if she could see along the next corridor and that was when she saw the writing on the wall.

TOUCH THE CRYSTAL WITH THE KEY

THIS WILL SET THE SPIRIT FREE

She reached into her bag for the crystal and felt an extraordinary feeling of warmth flowing through her body. She held the crystal in the palm of her hand and carefully touched it with the golden key. The crystal began to spin, faster and faster. Then a beautiful transformation took place. The crystal turned into a ball of purple light and floated slowly upwards, travelling at tremendous speed. It wove in and out of the bars of the iron gate then, without warning, it made straight for the opposite wall and flew right through it. For a few seconds, there was silence, then the noise of crashing and banging came from the spot through which the crystal had disappeared and the three children ran to the side of the tunnel to take cover. As the dust settled, the purple crystal appeared again and hovered in front of Molly as though it was trying to communicate with her and, at the same time, another crystal rolled beneath the gate and came to stop at her feet. From this second crystal, two names projected from it, cast as shadows on to the ground. Molly studied them and understood. She nodded at the purple crystal. She knew what had to be done. She reached for the key and touched this second crystal. This time a crimson light emerged, brilliant and sparkling, and flew towards the purple light that still hovered by Molly.

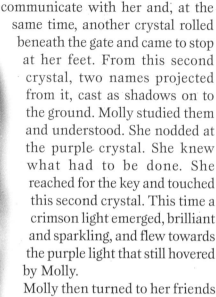

Molly then turned to her friends and said formally, "Allow me to introduce Beatrix and Alicia."

The two balls of light were flying round and round the children, flying between them and over their heads. Sarah and Jack started reaching up trying to catch them but Molly stopped them. "They will be eyes for us and guide us through this terrible place," she said. "I have this feeling when they come near me that gives me confidence and I know they are here to help us."

Molly's powers had increased steadily since she had first hung the key around her neck. She wasn't aware of that power then but anything for which she wished was likely to happen but there was one thing that it would not provide and that was the door through which they could escape. The evil power around them was still strong and would remain so until the last trace of the evil Peter had been destroyed. The fear that he was still alive remained with the children and it was this that forced them to hurry. The gate in front of them was still firmly shut. Jack and Sarah stood back so that Molly could try her magic powers to open it. The two balls of light had flown to the other side and now hovered at the limit of the children's sight. Molly stood in front of the gate

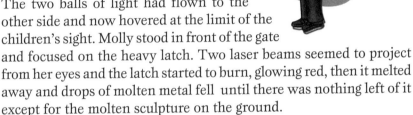

and focused on the heavy latch. Two laser beams seemed to project from her eyes and the latch started to burn, glowing red, then it melted away and drops of molten metal fell until there was nothing left of it except for the molten sculpture on the ground.

The children scrambled over the stones that littered the floor leading to the next tunnel.

"Don't you feel frightened to possess such power," Sarah asked Molly.

"No, I don't," Molly told her, "because I will only use the power for good."

The two lights flew towards them and spun in circles in front of them as if they were trying to impart a message.

"We must go to the right," Molly said. "The left passage is a dead end."

The two balls of light went in front of them. They would hover for a while and then set off as if they were jet driven until they were nearly out of sight and the three children would have to hurry to keep up with them. As they went further along the tunnel, the two lights started to fly quicker and quicker, repeatedly returning and flying around them before surging up the tunnel again. It was as if they were trying to make them go faster but they were going as fast as they could and they were tiring. Then Molly saw another door at the far end of the passage but it seemed a long, long way away and however fast they went, it didn't seem to be getting any nearer. Then Jack was running towards it and Molly was shouting at him, telling him to slow down and wait for them but the boy did not seem to hear. He rushed at the door and pushed it open and as it swung back, he went with it swinging in a wide arc. And he was hanging over a deep pit, a pit that had no bottom, that opened up beneath him like a huge abyss waiting to swallow him. Jack screamed, a scream that echoed around them and seemed to travel down all the tunnels through which they had come and back to them again. Fortunately he had the sense to hang on to the latch on the door and he was holding on to it for dear life for below him was the deep, dark shaft with no bottom in sight.

"Help, for God's sake help me. Get me out of here," he shouted. "I can't hang on much longer. I'm going to fall," And he kicked out frantically trying to swing back towards the girls as he felt his fingers beginning to slip.

The two girls ran to help him but they were too late. His fingers slipped down the length of the latch and Jack was falling, falling down into the emptiness beneath him and, as he fell, he screamed and the sound became fainter as he fell deeper and deeper.

Molly stood up and concentrated. She had to act quickly if she was going to save Jack. She pointed down into the shaft and lightning flashed from the tips of her fingers. The speed of light was the only thing that could save him now for his body was falling so quickly.

And then the sound changed from a screaming to a singing sound, a sound of relief, of happiness, the sound of singing. The two balls of light emerged first, twisting and turning, darting and dancing as they emerged from the shaft. Then Jack himself came floating up from the darkness as if he was being gently transported on a cushion of air.

"Welcome back, Jack," Sarah said. "Next time, look before you leap."

As Jack stepped back on to the firm ground there was a terrific crash and an iron door descended behind them with a roar that echoed like thunder all round them. They were all shocked by the suddenness of it. Sarah had been closest to it, had felt it brush against her clothes as it descended. If it had been any nearer it could have sliced her in two. She ran away from it and sheltered behind Molly.

"Do something, Molly. Let's get out of here. This dreadful place is getting to me. I can't and it. Can't you wish up a lift that will take us back to the real world or back to our own homes would be better."

As she was talking, the wooden door faded to be replaced by a glass one with numbers above it which read from one to eighty four. As they watched, mesmerised by all that was happening, the glass door slid back and came to halt with a loud ding and a voice said, "Mind the doors."

It was a lift, a lift with shining steel sides and roof and floor and a panel on the side with buttons which you had to press to direct it to the right floor.

"Wow, Molly, how did you do that."

"It just happened," Molly said. "I thought of a lift when you mentioned it and, well, there it was."

Jack was standing there staring at it in astonishment, his mouth wide open. Testing it out with the toe of his shoe.

"Come on then, don't stand round looking at it. Get in before it disappears again," and Sarah gave a Jack a shove towards it.

Molly took one look round, then she followed the other two with the two bright balls of light dancing round her head.

"Which floor do you want?" Sarah asked, looking at the buttons.

"That's strange, there are only two, up or down. I don't know, Sarah, I'll let you choose."

At that moment the sheet of metal began to rise slowly and they

43

could hear movement on the other side of it.

"Up, up," Sarah was almost screaming as she pressed the up button.

The door seemed to rise so slowly and all the time the iron barrier in front of them was steadily rising. Then with a whoosh the lift ascended at top speed and the children were pressed against the sides of the lift. Sarah had her eyes shut, praying that it would take them back to their own bedroom. Then the lift stopped and they could see through the glass door that they were back in a bedroom, but which one? The door slid back silently. The two balls of light were the first to leave. The children followed and, as they stepped out of it, the lift disappeared. Where it had been was just another wall. Sarah's first thought was the writing pad and she dashed to the bed to see if it was there. She prayed that it would be the one with the torn page. The pad was there and she picked it up, then she threw it back on the bed in disgust. "Stupid thing," she moaned.

"What happened back there?" Jack asked. "What was behind that door."

"It was him. It had to be. We've got to find these other crystals. That's the only way we're going to get out of here. Beatrix, Alicia," Molly called.

There was no sign of them.

"They must have gone through the door," Jack said, and went across and opened it, revealing yet another tunnel. "Come on then."

They had only gone a few steps when they spotted the two balls of light, darting and dancing between the stones. They seemed excited about something. The three children ran towards them but the crystals had disappeared into the wall by the time they reached them. Then they tumbled out through the roof and, at the same time, another crystal fell into Molly's hands. She touched it with the golden key and immediately it turned into a ball of light of the most beautiful, translucent pink. It lifted from Molly's hand and flew to the wall where, in glistening letters, it wrote the name Catherine.

"Welcome Catherine," Molly said and the three balls of light flew round in great excitement.

"I wish they could speak," Sarah said.

As she spoke, the three crystals took off at high speed down the tunnel and the children ran after them, wondering if the crystals had sped off at that speed because there was something evil behind them. But then they came back and started flying round Molly's head. The children stopped, trying to work out the message that they were trying to convey. Beatrix bobbed up and down vigorously in front of her as if she had touched a nerve.

"You wait here," Jack told Molly and Sarah. "I will go with her," and he ran after the flying balls of light until he was out of sight. Within seconds though he was running back, waving his arms and shouting at them, "Quick, get back to their bedroom. Don't stand there. RUN. There's ...no.....time....to lose."

"Oh my God," Sarah screamed.

From the depths of the tunnel, they could see the great hairy spider emerging, the spider that had accosted them before. It's jaws were snapping and he was right behind Jack. He had almost reached the boy. The girls had already reached the bedroom and were shouting encouragement to Jack. The three balls whizzed in over their heads but Jack was tiring and the spider was gaining on him with its huge, menacing strides. The girls were screaming at him to hurry and they reached out and dragged him through the door as the spider lunged at him. They slammed the door shut, using all their force to do so and trapping the tips of the spider's feelers as they probed towards them.

"We can't hold it," Sarah almost sobbed. "It's too strong for us."

The spider was pushing against the door screaming partly in anger and partly in pain and it was shaking with the force of his fury. Then, behind the children came the repetitive voice, "Mind the doors."

Glancing over her shoulder,

Molly saw the shining steel of the open lift.

"Quick," she said, "get in it."

The three crystals were already flying round and round inside it. The children made a dash for it with Sarah springing at the down button, pressing it time and time again, willing the lift to descend as the spider burst through the door and made a dash for the lift. But it was too late. The doors shut silently and the lift descended. The children sank to the floor. "I wonder where we'll finish up now," Sarah said.

"Well we've got three crystals now. There's only six to go."

"I don't mind that," Sarah said slowly," as long as we don't meet any more spiders." Sarah couldn't stand spiders.

The lift took them down to yet another tunnel. The crystals flew out first and sped up and down the corridor before hovering in front of the open lift.

"Come on," said Molly. "They're telling us its safe."

They all, stood in the tunnel wondering which way to go. The tunnel seemed endless in each direction.

"I don't think my legs will take me another step," Sarah groaned.

"What we need is something to ride on," Molly thought. She told the other two to move to the side of the tunnel and wished for something to help them, holding the key tightly and with her eyes shut.

"What on earth is this coming for us now," Sarah almost screamed.

Jack looked as though he was going to run away from it.

"It's alright. Stay where you are," Molly ordered.

Whoosh - something like a metal snake sped past them and then came back the other way.

"It's a monorail. I've heard about them," Jack said.

There was something coming along the line towards them, something that rumbled and the rumbling echoed along the tunnel, sounding like a lot of people talking.

"It's the train," Sarah shouted.

It came to a halt in front of them and two glass doors slid silently open.

"All aboard," Molly ordered. "Come on, no time to waste."

As they sat down, the doors closed and the train set off. They seemed to be riding for a long time but then they saw a light ahead and it seemed they were coming to the end of the tunnel and the three crystals were becoming excited. The train drew slowly to a stop and, as the doors opened, the crystals flew out. There were stone steps leading down from the train which the children went down. As soon as they reached the ground, the train and the mono rail disappeared. There were more stone steps in front of them. The crystals had already flown up them and now the children followed. They seemed never ending and they wondered if they would ever reach the top. Then Beatrix flew back towards them and started whizzing round Molly's head.

"You've found the next crystal," Molly exclaimed and Beatrix bobbed up and down in front of her as if to tell her that she had. "Come on then, we must follow her."

"It's alright for them," Sarah groaned. "They can fly. I wish I could."

"So do I," Molly told her and, at that instant, they were all lifted off their feet and they were floating, floating up the flight of stairs until they had reached the top where, once again, they found themselves standing.

"That was fantastic," Jack said, "what a wonderful feeling!"

There was another door in front of them, which Molly opened cautiously and there was another bedroom in front of them. Sarah pushed past her and made straight for the writing pad on the bed, but there was no page torn from it. It was the wrong room. Thunder and lightning was apparent outside the window darkening the room.

Beatrix flew round their heads, then flew towards the wardrobe and disappeared through it.

"That's strange," Molly said.

"Yes it is. Don't you remember Jack, Molly moved the wardrobe at the last room we were in to let us out."

"And you told us Jack that all the bedrooms acted in the same way so....."

"He probably moved it back to confuse us," Jack said. "That's how his mind works."

The three crystals reappeared but they stayed dancing round the wardrobe.

"We've got to look behind it," Molly said, so they pulled it out from the wall and, there , behind it, was another hole.

"Shall we go?" Molly asked.

"You bet," Sarah said as she pushed through but the crystals went past her at speed. Zip, zip. The other two followed but Molly turned and cast a spell so that the wardrobe slid back in place.

This tunnel was not built the same as the others. It was rough cut, the sort of tunnel you would find in a gold mine. There were still flamed torches lining the way but the light from the flying crystals would have been enough. The tunnel rose upwards and it was very dusty.

"What I would give for a burger and a big coke," Sarah said.

"So would I" said Molly, "a real cold one." But they were interrupted once again by the crystals who returned and flew round and round them again. "Come on, we've got to follow them."

They arrived at the foot of more stone steps, leading steeply upwards and, on the second step embedded in the stone, was the fourth crystal, showing as a golden glow. Molly touched it with the key and immediately it rose up into the atmosphere. It shone like the sun itself, glowing golden against the darkness of the tunnel. Then it flew towards the other crystals and joined with them into one large ball of light which had changed colour into a beautiful emerald green. Then it split into four again and whizzed round and round as if they were celebrating their freedom. Then they slowed down and fused into one ball again and flying down until it hovered in front of Molly.

"Thankyou, Molly, for all you have done for us." It spoke in a gentle voice.

"You can speak," said Molly. "It's so nice to hear your voice."

"Molly, this is Beatrix speaking. I want to introduce you to Karina and the letter K. Your first word is now complete. Then she asked if all three children would touch the green light. Each placed their hands inside it.

"Now, I want you to concentrate and clear your minds, Can you see us now as our true selves."

The children were all smiling.

"If you ever need us, we will be there," Beatrix told them. We can fuse together in no time at all. But we must go now. Evil is very close behind you and we must be away." They split into four separate balls of light and sped away up the steps.

The children were alone. What had Beatrix meant. Had the spider broken through and pursued them. Beatrix's voice came down to them. "You haven't a minute to lose. You must go. Something evil is advancing up the steps behind you. A strong, wooden door is ahead of you and it leads to an arena. You must reach it but hurry, hurry, hurry," and her voice faded gradually away.

It didn't take them long to reach the door. It took the strength of the three children to turn and pull the heavy latch and then they were through. They found themselves in a large, round hall with five doors spaced equally round its perimeter. The door through which they had entered slammed shut behind them but not before the balls of light had reappeared and followed them into the hall. Now they flew round and round, hovering over each door as if they were scanning it. Then they disappeared through different doors and the children stood and waited, wondering from which door the evil one was likely to emerge, wishing the crystals would come back and let them know.

Zip, zip, zip, three of the crystals had returned but there was no sign of the fourth. Then the three of them made for the fifth door. Molly stared at the fourth one. Surely the other crystal should have returned by now. What was happening behind that one?

The three crystals were back now, circling round and round Molly, forcing her to move towards the fourth door. Then the fifth door began vibrating until, with a crash, it broke away from its hinges and fell to the ground. Outstretched tentacles reached into the hall and started to feel their way round the walls at first, then towards the children. Molly was mesmerised by them. She stared at them quite unable to move. Then one of the tentacles caught hold of her leg, groping, winding until it had firm hold of her and then it started to drag her towards the doorway. She tried to struggle free but two more tentacles weaved in her direction and took hold of her arms.

"Jack, Jack," she was screaming. "Rescue me. I can't move," but Jack felt as helpless as she was. What could he do? For a moment Molly's mind cleared and she remembered what Beatrix had told her and she called out for her and, at the same time, the key escaped from its hold and fell to the ground. The octopus like creature saw it first. He let go of one of Molly's arms and made a grab for the key. The crystals were flying round Molly. She was half in the corridor and half in the hall now, still struggling to escape and screaming at the top of her voice. The creature had turned Molly on to her back and was disappearing down the steps, dragging Molly behind it. Then Molly took a deep breath. She must not panic. Her brain began to function. She looked round for a weapon to defend herself. Star Wars sprang to mind. That was the answer and the next second she found herself holding a laser rod.

"Come on then," she shouted at the creature who was dragging her and lashed out as she fought for her life, striking first this way, then the other until she cut right through one of his long arms. It loosened its hold on her and Molly managed to wriggle out of his grip and scramble spoke

back up the stairs and into the hall. The creature was roaring and screaming both with anger and from the pain that Molly had inflicted. Still roaring it charged out into the arena and Molly attacked it again, cutting off another of its long, prehensile arm. It pulled back, still screaming.

Jack and Sarah were pushing hard on the fourth door and, as it opened, the three of them dashed through it. Molly turned to seal it behind them with a quick gesture of her magic. There were more steps in front of them going upwards as far as the eye could see. They started to climb.

"I've never seen so many steps in my life," Sarah moaned.

As they climbed there was a rumbling sound behind them and the steps they had climbed crumbled behind them and the stones fell into a deep, dark abyss.

"I don't like the look of this. We must move. Before these steps start to crumble as well."

The tried to go faster but they were all tired but at last they were standing at the top with the crystals flying round their heads and the sound of the falling stairs reverberating around them. The fourth crystal had rejoined them and Molly was pleased to see that she was safe.

The four crystals fused together and started to speak. "Molly dear," they said, "Katherine has located the fifth crystal and the labyrinth is destroying itself."

"But what's causing it," Molly interrupted.

"We'll explain later but the important thing now is to keep moving. We must go quickly. That creature back there will have changed into something else and it won't be far behind."

They started along the tunnel with the debris and the noise of the falling masonry still following them.

"I think the tunnel is going to collapse," Jack said with despair in his voice. "I'm sure it is," and at that moment the ground began to shake violently and large pieces of stone fell from the walls alongside them. They had to do something quickly. They could not run fast enough to escape.

Molly touched the key, concentrating on asking for help and, suddenly the three children found themselves further along the tunnel with the noise and dust of the falling masonry a long way behind them.

"Phew, what happened there," Jack said in wonder, but they had no time to stop and wonder. Whatever was back along the tunnel was still advancing, still drawing closer to them. In front of them, the crystals were weaving in and out, excited at something they had found.

"It's the fifth crystal. I just know it is," Molly said. "I wonder what it's name is."

And there it was, embedded in the stone wall. Molly took the key out quickly and released the crystal. The four others were hovering round and the new crystal flew up to meet them. It was a beautiful sapphire blue and it shone with brilliance as it fused with the others.

"Molly dear, "We now have Doreen with us but we have alarming news. You can see that the tunnel is caving in behind us but the whole labyrinth is in danger of collapsing. It is only a matter of time before it is all destroyed. We must move fast."

"But we haven't found the other crystals," Molly said.

"We know. Every moment is precious. The evil one is even more determined to get hold of the key now that his creation is falling apart. He'll use any means to get what he wants. Come," and the crystals darted in front of them as if they were urging them forwards.

There was another flight of steps for them to climb and each step seemed steeper than the last one. They climbed as quickly as they could but there was no way they could keep up with the balls of light that were now hovering at the top. As the children climbed up the last step, Jack recognised where they were. Doors were positioned along each side of a long corridor and he knew they were near the bedroom they were seeking. They all fixed their eyes on the door at the end of the corridor.

"I'm sure that's the one we want, come on," Sarah called and raced towards the door but the crystals were already there and had disappeared through the door.

The children pushed the door together and rushed into the bedroom. Sarah made for the bed and seized the writing pad that was on it. "It's the right one," she called out. "We're in the right room," and she started to dance holding the pad aloft. Molly was dancing too and the girls held each others hands and danced round and round until they were dizzy and collapsed on the bed to regain their breath. Then

Molly looked at Jack. He didn't seem pleased. He looked miserable and she asked him what was wrong.

"I'll start to age as soon as I leave this place," Jack told them. "I won't be a boy any longer."

"But we've got to get out," Molly said. "Any chance is a chance worth taking but we've got to find the other crystals."

Then, looking round she asked where the five crystals were.

"They flew through the wardrobe while you two were dancing around," Jack told her.

Molly immediately cast a spell towards the cupboard and it slid to one side, revealing a hole, just big enough for one person to go through it at a time. Molly looked through it and called out the names of the crystals, one after the other but there was no sign of them.

"They'll be back," Jack said, "I know they will."

Then they were suddenly there and flying round and round the room. They slowed down and collected in one large colourful ball.

Molly went and put her hands on the wall. She felt frustrated. They were so near her own bedroom where they would be safe and yet they couldn't get through to it. She banged the wall in frustration but at that moment, - zip, zip, zip, zip, zip, the five crystals flew through the hole in the wall.

"You're back," Molly exclaimed with relief.

The crystals united in one glowing ball and Beatrix spoke.

"We're sorry if we worried you, dear but we have news for you. We have located the other four crystals but one of you will have to go and collect them. It is beyond our powers."

Molly stared at her in consternation. Whoever went for the crystals would be taking a terrible risk. The tunnels were breaking up. There was a chance that whoever went after the other crystals would be unable to get back. And of course the evil one was still skulking in the shadows. He could be anywhere and in any form. The dangers were extreme but one of them would have to go.

"I've got no choice," Molly said. "One of us will have to go. Time's running out. I'm going in."

"Molly, you can't. It's too dangerous," Sarah put out her hand to stop her.

"Sarah's right," Jack said. "It's far too dangerous for you. I know my way better than you," and he gently pulled Molly back.

"May we make a suggestion dear," Beatrix's voice floated across the room. "If Jack is willing to go, then Sabrina and Katherine will go with him. Jack can take your bag and put the crystals in that,"

Molly agreed and Jack made for the hole with the two crystals flying in front of him, Leading the way. It was very quiet when he had gone. Nobody spoke and not a sound came from the other side of the wall. They seemed to have been away for ages and Molly was getting worried when there was a terrific explosion. The whole bedroom shook. Blocks of stone were hurled into the room and the heavy door broke off its hinges and fell to the ground with a crash.

The two girls threw themselves on to the ground beside the bed, trying to shelter from the flying debris. Then the noise quietened down and everything became still again except for the occasional stone that still rolled across the floor. The crystals emerged from the top drawer of the dressing table where they had hidden. There was no sight or sound of Jack. He had been gone for ages and Molly was getting worried. Something had alerted the crystals. How Molly wished they could tell her what was happening but they could only talk when they welded together in a ball. They were bobbing up and down in front of her as if they were trying to make her understand. Then Jack's head appeared through the hole. It was streaked with dirt but he was grinning.

"I've got something for you," he said.

"Thank goodness you're safe," Molly said with relief.

"I've got all the other crystals," and he handed the bag to Molly.

By this time the two crystals had flown through the hole and welded with the others to make a big, colourful ball.

Jack's body began to follow his head as he started to scramble through the hole. But, at that moment, two huge claws fastened over his shoulders and started to pull him backwards.

"Quick, Molly," he called, "take the bag. Here, be quick," and he started to struggle, trying to escape from this roaring creature screamed with fury as he tried to pull Jack out of the hole and seize the bag.

Molly grabbed it just in time. She thrust the key into the bag and four colourful balls of light emerged, each one a different shade and a different colour. They flew up and joined the ball until it became twice its size.

Jack was shouting for the girls to get out while they could. Beatrix in her soft voice.

"Molly dear, I'm afraid there is no time to waste. We will have to do what Jack is telling us."

"NO," shouted Molly, "no, we can't leave him," but there was no time.

The crystals had flown down to the wall where the girls had first emerged. They stood in line, each one projecting a letter to make a word. Molly couldn't understand what it said.

"Molly, you have to say it backwards," Sarah shouted. "It's a mirror image. Just do it. Be quick."

The bedroom began to vibrate. Then they heard thunder so loud that it drowned the sound of Jack's screams.

Molly was disturbed. She wanted to get back to reality but she didn't want to leave Jack behind. Sarah was urging her to hurry. She pointed the key at the wall and recited the words that the crystals had made.

"ME FOR DOOR A MAKE YOU DEMAND I,
KEY THE HOLDER OF AM I"

Whoosh. The door appeared straight away. Then a big brass lock took its place. Molly carefully put the golden key into it and turned it.

"Push, push, push," Sarah chanted, dancing up and down impatiently.

Slowly the door creaked open. The nine crystals were the first through it, then Sarah. Molly went to follow but she paused and looked behind. Her eyes filled with tears. She could only think of Jack. Then she heard him.

"Molly, wait for me."

That was the voice she longed to hear. Jack came stumbling through the hole.

"You're safe," she said, wiping away the tears with the back of her hand. She reached out to take his hand and pull him with her and, as her hand touched his, he began to change. He turned into an ugly creature so slowly. Molly wanted to get away from him but she couldn't. She was mesmerised by what was happening in front of her. His nose grew long and his ears became pointed. His body changed shape and his eyes were bloodshot and calculating and the hand that she was holding changed into claws, claws that grabbed hold of her wrists and held her tight.

"I'm going to take your soul. Do you hear me. Your body can rot away in here. You stole my key and I am here to take it back. The world is mine," and he laughed, an evil laugh that sent shivers down Molly's spine.

At the sound of his laugh, the nine crystals came flying back into the room and they bombarded this creature, coming at him time and time again. He was forced to let go of Molly as he struck out at these brilliant balls of light. Then, with a strangled scream, he fell to the ground and behind him stood Jack, the real Jack, with a big rock in his hand.

"Oh, Jack," Molly said. "Are you alright?"

"I've a few bruises but I'll live. Let's get out of here before the whole place falls down."

They made their way through into the bedroom and, as they went in, the door faded and disappeared. They were back in her own bedroom. The two girls were in their dressing gowns and her mother was shouting up the stairs telling them to settle down and go to sleep that instance and, as for Jack, he was studying his face in the mirror to see if any wrinkles were appearing.

"Do I look alright?" He asked the girls.

"You look alright to me," Sarah said, "but I don't know about your clothes," and she started to giggle. "Don't worry," she added when she saw the look on his face. "My brothers have got some clothes that will fit you. We'll sort it out in the morning."

The ball of light was hovering over the bed.

"Molly dear," said Beatrix's voice. "Will you do one last thing for us. Touch us with the golden key just once more."

Molly did as they asked and touched the globe of light. It glowed very brightly and then, puff, it broke into nine pieces and the pieces became white witches, nine beautiful witches standing in a circle all with smooth skin and long golden hair and there was a feeling of love and peace all round them. They all looked the same except that each one had different coloured clothes.

"Well, my dear," Beatrix said, "we must leave you now. We have a lot of work to do." Then she pointed at the window and the lower pane lifted, leaving a space through which each of them flew, zip, zip, zip, zip, zip, zip, zip, zip, zip.

Molly stood at the window and waved to each of them as they

flew up into the starlit sky.

"I'm going to miss them," Sarah said. "I hope we'll see them again."

"It looks as though you'll have to stay with us, Jack," said Molly.

Jack sat on the bed and buried his head in his hands. He looked as though he was going to cry. Molly put her arms round his shoulders to comfort him.

"You're alright, Jack," she told him." You haven't changed a bit honest. You look just the same."

"I don't know about you two," Sarah said, "but I'm starving. I don't feel as if I've eaten for days."

"You'll have to wait until my parents have gone to bed. Then I'll go down and find something," Molly told her and it wasn't long before they heard her parents coming upstairs and going into their room. Molly crept down and came back with some biscuits and three cans of coke.

Sarah seized a couple of biscuits and one of the cans but Jack just stared at her. He had never seen anyone drinking from a can before.

Molly had to show him how to open his and drink from it. He took a mouthful and grinned. "I think I'll like it here," he said.

And it was at that moment that they heard a bang, a bang that echoed round the room and it had come from the other side of the room. It was then that Molly explained why the labyrinth collapsed around them. Peter turned each crystal into part of it. One by one as they entered to look for Jack. As the crystals were released in turn, the labyrinth destroyed itself.

Sarah hid her head in her sleeping bag. Molly and Jack stared at each other in horror. Was evil Peter still alive? Was he on the other side of the wall, trying to get through to them?

Jack crept across to the wall and put his ear to it. There was more banging on the other side, banging and rumbling. "I think I know what it is," he said. "I think it's the stones settling down. They looked at each other. Dare they go back through the door and see if that is what was really happening without the crystals to guide them?

"I don't know about you two," Sarah said, "but I've had enough excitement for one day. I'm going to get some shut eye and see what things are like in the morning," and she snuggled down under the bedclothes.

Molly was smothering a yawn. She suddenly felt very tired. She pulled out the spare duvet for Jack, then she tumbled into bed beside Sarah and fell fast asleep. The three of them slept deeply. Molly was the first to wake. The sun was shining through the bedroom window. Sarah was sound asleep but Jack was tossing and turning and mumbling something that sounded as if he was talking about the wardrobe. Molly shook him awake. He sat up and told them that they must look at the wardrobe. They had not put it back in front of the hole. Evil Peter could still reach them.

Molly shook him. "Tell me this is only a dream," she said. "Tell me this isn't really happening."

Jack sat on the floor and shook his head. "I don't know anything any more," he said.

That was when the bedroom door flew open and there was Mr Perkins standing there demanding to know what was going on. He glowered at Jack sitting on the floor.

"It's not what you think, Dad," Molly said, "really it isn't," and she started explaining everything that had happened.

Mrs Perkins had come upstairs and she had come into the bed

room too. She had looked astonished at the sight of Jack sitting on the floor wrapped up in their spare duvet but she seemed even more astonished as Molly's long story unfolded.

Then Jack piped up. "Mr Perkins," he said. "What Molly is trying to say is that this hole in the wall couldn't have happened by anything that you would have considered normal."

Then Sarah joined in and started describing the crystals and their beautiful colours.

Mr and Mrs Perkins looked at the three of them dubiously. They had never heard such a tale in their lives and they didn't know what to think. Especially a big gaping hole in the wall.

"It's true Mum," Molly said. "The key really has given me some magic powers. Just watch the dressing tables," and she turned to it, touched the key with her hand and concentrated. Immediately the furniture began to lift off the floor.

"Put it back, Molly, straight away," her mother said. "You'll break something."

"Come on," said Mr Perkins, pulling his wife after him. "We're not going to stay here, not with all these going ons. He must move us somewhere else straight away."

"You children get yourself up and washed," Mrs Perkins told the three of them "while your Dad goes round and sees his boss. We're not staying here."

By the time the three children had finished their breakfast, Mr Perkins, looking red faced and indignant was back in the kitchen. Mr Bradley, his boss was there too and he made the children repeat every word of their story. Then he said, "You're quite right, Perkins, you can't carry on living here, Now I'll tell you what I propose and that is that you'll come and live with us. We've got a house that's far too big for the two of us and my wife hasn't been too well lately. So if Mrs Perkins could cope with the cooking, we can be one family. We haven't any children of our own, so you'll be like our grandchildren because you must come as well Jack and I've no doubt we'll see Sarah from time to time."

"Lots and lots," Sarah said happily.

"How about it then, Perkins?" Mr Bradley asked.

Molly's father hesitated but her mother thought it was a lovely idea and said they'd love to come.

"Right," said Mr Bradley, "we'll have the van round this afternoon, two o'clock. I will get someone to cement up that hole as well."

Well the week was certainly busy for the Perkins and Jack, of course, and Sarah helped. They had several journeys to make with all their belongings. It was on the last trip that Molly and Sarah looked back at the old street as they pulled away. Flashbacks of old Mrs Towers and the adventures they had had sprung to mind. Their house grew smaller and then disappeared completely from view as they turned the corner. They were busy unpacking their belongings but then, Molly felt this warm feeling filling her body and she knew that she still held the magic powers. She still had one score to settle. Grinning at Sarah, she slowly turned herself into and old, old lady. Holding Sarah's arm for support, the two of them set off for the school. They knew they would find Chunky nearby. That was where he looked for and found his victims.

"There he is, Moll," Sarah said. "Go on smack him one with your power.

"No Sarah. Violence doesn't solve anything. If I did that, I would only be bringing myself down to his level."

"Shhhh, here he comes," Sarah hissed..

Chunky had spied two victims that would give him a lot of pleasure to taunt, an old lady and a young girl. He approached them in a menacing way, a fashionable base ball cap on his head. Molly was waiting for him. As he came alongside her, she purposely knocked into him.

"Hello young man," she said. "Can you spare a few pence?"

"Buzz off, you old witch," he answered. "Do I look stupid?"

"You haven't learned your lesson yet, have you?"

"Here, what are you babbling on about. Get out of my way," and he pushed her roughly to one side.

"Does the name of Molly Perkins mean anything to you?" she asked.

Immediately his hand went up to touch the peak of his base ball cap. That name had been haunting him for the last few days. He had done everything he could think of to erase it and hide it.

"Here, how do you know what's on..... Just mind your own business, witch. Now buzz off."

"Well, he got that part right," said Sarah.

He pushed off and marched up the road with the peak of his cap pulled down hard over his eyes. Molly followed him and Sarah wasn't far behind. Chunky was walking quickly and the girls found it difficult to keep up with him. He lead them along one road and turned down the road into which Molly and her family had moved. The girls hid behind a parked car and watched where he went.

"I don't believe this," said Molly. "We've moved in immediately opposite Chunky Hill."

It was when they were eating sandwiches and drinking coke in their own kitchen that they heard shouting from the road and the three children ran out to see what was happening. George Hill was in the garden with a man who must have been his father and this man was knocking Chunky about and shouting at him and Chunky was trying to get away from him but he didn't have a chance.

Molly felt sorry for the boy.

"The big bully", she said, perhaps louder than she had meant to.

The man heard her and spun round. "Mind your own business," he shouted, "and don't poke your nose into other people's," and he pushed his nose with his finger to emphasise the point he was making. Molly twitched her own nose at the man and immediately his

finger stuck to his nose. He started to shout and swear as he tried to pull the finger away but that only seemed to hold it more firmly in place.

Molly lifted from the ground and flew across the road and stood beside Chunky.

"Aren't you that girl - I took your...."

"Forget it," Molly said. I think you've come off worse than me to look at you. My name is Molly Perkins."

Straight away, Chunky's hand went up to his forehead.

"Don't worry," Molly said. "I have taken it off. Now you, just promise me that you'll never bully anyone else again, ever."

Chunky stood and stared at her and he felt ashamed. "I promise," he said.

"Are you alright, Moll?" Sarah shouted from across the street.

"We certainly are," Molly shouted back, "aren't we Chunky?"

"George," he said. "My real name's George. Could you do something for my Dad. He'll really go for me if he gets upset."

The man still had his finger stuck to his nose, which had slowly been growing longer and must have been a full eight inches long. "My dose, my dose," he was groaning.

Molly went across to him and spoke to him. Slowly his nose went back to its normal size and his hand dropped back to his side. Molly told him that if he ever hit another child, then his nose would grow again but next time it would be longer still. Then she went back to her own house and her own friends and, as they finished their drinks and sandwiches, she felt the last of the magic powers draining away from her. She put her hand to the chain round her neck. It was there but there was nothing on it. The golden key had vanished.

Has Molly lost her power? Has the key gone forever? Find out in the next adventure of Molly Perkins.